To every child that is,
was and will be,

This story was written
for your heart from me.

Let us be Sisters
and let us be Brothers,

Let us be Holden
to each of each other.

Holden Hugs The World
Written & Illustrated By Jon Marro

Independently Published By:

WORLDS WITHIN

Worlds Within Enterprises, LLC
www.worldswithinbooks.org

Ordering Information:
For information about special discounts for bulk purchases and wholesale, please contact the publisher at the website address listed above.

Lovingly edited by Blair Wojcik, Irene Tsouprake & Eva Ackerman.

Special Thanks to my Hug Wear Ninjas Jess & Alex for helping to inspire Holden, and to Butch Leiber for holding such creative space and being Holden's first hug in the world.

Printed by Ingram Spark (www.ingramspark.com) in the United States of America.

First Printing: 2019

ISBN 978-1-7341906-9-4 (Paperback)

ISBN 978-1-7341906-4-9 (Hardcover)

ISBN 978-1-7341906-8-7 (eBook)

Holden Hugs The World

Written and Illustrated By

JON MARRO♡

There once was a Being
whose soul was quite golden,

He loved hugging SO much,
that his Mom named him Holden.

Holden held tight to his known Universe,

Until one day on Earth things began to get worse.

When Earth needed help
it called out for some Love,

So Holden went down and gave Earth a hug.

He hugged
colorful birds

and deep
rooted trees,

He hugged snow-covered mountains

and hard-working bees.

He hugged the crookedest rivers

and calm, quiet lakes,

He hugged all the elephants

and even the snakes.

He hugged a lost polar bear
and the fast melting ice,

He gave hugs for a moment

and hugs that would last,

**But before he hugged anyone,
Holden made sure to ask!**

He hugged people of all faiths,
all colors and ages,

He hugged people who earned
all sorts of wages.

He hugged those who were different
and those quite the same,

The one-of-a-kind snowflakes
and each drop of rain.

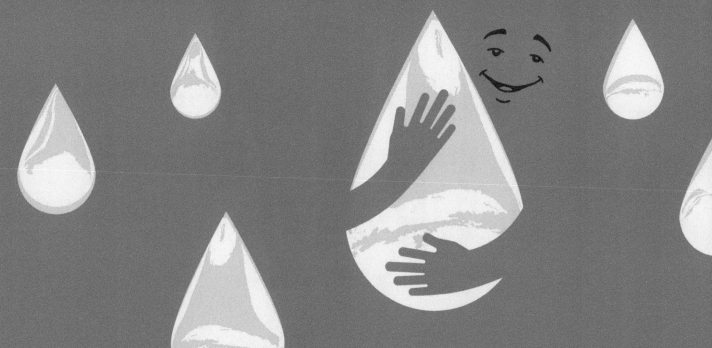

He hugged the lives
that were new,

And those
that were long.

**Holden's hugs felt like music
to the sweetest of songs.**

**He hugged those who tried hard
to give it their best,**

**And he hugged those who needed
to lie down and rest.**

Holden hugged people's prayers and he hugged people's thoughts,

He hugged the food
that they grew

and the things
that they bought.

He hugged the whole world
before it was too late.

Now that Holden had held
each and every thing nearer,

The purpose for living on Earth
became clearer.

He spread lots of Love
across this planet of ours,

Then looked up to see
a new friend in the stars.

The two hugged
each other as
they giggled
with glee...

I'm Holden You
and You're
Holden Me!